TRaMPOLiNE

GYMNASTICS GOALBOOK

Contents:

Gymnastics Info:

Name: _______________________________________

Age: _______________________________________

Level: _______________________________________

Club: _______________________________________

Coach/es: _______________________________________

Favourite skill/s: _______________________________________

____

Favourite trampoline event/s: _______________________________________

____

Favourite Olympic gymnast: _______________________________________

____

Favourite training outfit: _______________________________________

Inspirational words or quotes:

Inspirational words or quotes:

My Yearly Training Goals:

Date: _______________

____

____

____

____

____

____

____

____

____

____

____

◇   You can do it!   ◇

My Yearly Training Outcomes:

Date: _______________

____

____

____

____

____

____

____

____

____

____

____

◇　Go for gold!　◇

My Yearly Training Goals:

Date: _______________

____

____

____

____

____

____

____

____

____

____

____

◇ Dreams are possible. ◇

My Yearly Training Outcomes:

Date: _________________

____

____

____

____

____

____

____

____

____

____

____

◇ Flipping out is fun! ◇

My Training Goals:

Date: _______________

____

____

____

____

____

____

____

____

____

____

____

◇ Don't give up! ◇

My Training Outcomes:

Date: _______________

My Training Goals:

Date: _______________

____

____

____

____

____

____

____

____

____

____

____

◇   Aim high!   ◇

My Training Outcomes:

Date: ___________________

____

____

____

____

____

____

____

____

____

____

____

◇ You're a star! ◇

My Training Goals:

Date: _______________

◇ *If you don't try — you won't know* ◇
what you're actually capable of.

My Training Outcomes:

Date: _________________

My Training Goals:

Date: _______________

My Training Outcomes:

Date: _______________

My Training Goals:

Date: ______________

My Training Outcomes:

Date: _______________

____

____

____

____

____

____

____

____

____

____

____

◇ Be flexible, be strong. And smile! ◇

My Training Goals:

Date: __________________

My Training Outcomes:

Date: _______________

____

____

____

____

____

____

____

____

____

____

____

My Training Goals:

Date: _________________

My Training Outcomes:

Date: _______________

____

____

____

____

____

____

____

____

____

____

____

____

◇ Flipping out is fun! ◇

My Training Goals:

Date: ______________

My Training Outcomes:

Date: _______________

My Training Goals:

Date: _______________

◇   Aim high!   ◇

My Training Outcomes:

Date: ______________

◇ You're a star! ◇

My Training Goals:

Date: _______________

◇ Trampolining counts as flying. ◇

My Training Outcomes:

Date: _______________

My Training Goals:

Date: _______________

____

____

____

____

____

____

____

____

____

____

____

◇ *If you don't try — you won't know*
what you're actually capable of. ◇

My Training Outcomes:

Date: _______________

My Training Goals:

Date: ______________________

My Training Outcomes:

Date: _______________

My Training Goals:

Date: _______________

My Training Outcomes:

Date: _______________

____

____

____

____

____

____

____

____

____

____

____

◇ Fly like an eagle. ◇

My Training Goals:

Date: _______________

You're amazing.

My Training Outcomes:

Date: _______________

My Training Goals:

Date: _______________

My Training Outcomes:

Date: ___________________

My Training Goals:

Date: ______________________

My Training Outcomes:

Date: ________________

My Training Goals:

Date: _________________

____
____
____
____
____
____
____
____
____
____
____
____

◇ Dreams are possible. ◇

My Training Outcomes:

Date: _______________

____

____

____

____

____

____

____

____

____

____

____

◇ **Flipping out is fun!** ◇

My Training Goals:

Date: _______________

My Training Outcomes:

Date: _______________

My Training Goals:

Date: _______________

My Training Outcomes:

Date: _______________

My Training Goals:

Date: _______________

____

____

____

____

____

____

____

____

____

____

____

◇ Trampolining counts as flying. ◇

My Training Outcomes:

Date: _______________

◇ I love trampolining! ◇

My Training Goals:

Date: _______________

◇ *If you don't try — you won't know*
what you're actually capable of. ◇

My Training Outcomes:

Date: _______________

My Training Goals:

Date: _______________

◇ Trampolining is the best! ◇

My Training Outcomes:

Date: _______________

My Training Goals:

Date: _______________

My Training Outcomes:

Date: _____________________

____

____

____

____

____

____

____

____

____

____

____

◇ Trampolining counts as flying. ◇

My Training Goals:

Date: _______________

My Training Outcomes:

Date: ________________

My Training Goals:

Date: _______________

My Training Outcomes:

Date: _________________

____

____

____

____

____

____

____

____

____

____

____

◇ Be flexible, be strong. And smile! ◇

My Training Goals:

Date: _______________

My Training Outcomes:

Date: _______________

____

____

____

____

____

____

____

____

____

____

____

____

◇　　Go for gold!　　◇

My Training Goals:

Date: _______________

My Training Outcomes:

Date: _______________

My Training Goals:

Date: _______________

My Training Outcomes:

Date: _______________

My Competition Goals:

Date: _______________

Competition name: _______________

____

____

____

____

____

____

____

____

____

____

COMMENTS: _______________

____

My Competition Achievements:

Date: _______________

Competition name: ___________________

____

____

____

____

____

____

____

____

____

SCORES: _______________________

____

My Competition Goals:

Date: _______________

Competition name: _______________

____

____

____

____

____

____

____

____

____

____

COMMENTS: _______________

____

My Competition Achievements:

Date: _______________

Competition name: _______________

____

____

____

____

____

____

____

____

____

SCORES: _______________________

____

◇   you got this!   ◇

My Competition Goals:

Date: ___________________

Competition name: ___________________

____

____

____

____

____

____

____

____

____

____

COMMENTS: ___________________________

____

◇ Trampolining is the best! ◇

My Competition Achievements:

Date: _______________

Competition name: _______________

____

____

____

____

____

____

____

____

____

____

SCORES: _______________

____

◇ **Don't forget to have fun.** ◇

My Competition Goals:

Date: _______________

Competition name: _______________

____

____

____

____

____

____

____

____

____

____

COMMENTS: _______________

____

 **Run towards a challenge, not away from it.**

My Competition Achievements:

Date: _______________

Competition name: _______________________

____

____

____

____

____

____

____

____

____

SCORES: _________________________________

____

My Competition Goals:

Date: _________________

Competition name: _________________

____

____

____

____

____

____

____

____

____

____

COMMENTS: _______________________________

____

◇ You're amazing. ◇

My Competition Achievements:

Date: _______________

Competition name: _______________

____

____

____

____

____

____

____

____

____

____

SCORES: _______________

____

My Competition Goals:

Date: _______________

Competition name: _______________

____

____

____

____

____

____

____

____

____

COMMENTS: _______________

____

My Competition Achievements:

Date: _______________________

Competition name: ____________________________

____

____

____

____

____

____

____

____

____

____

SCORES: ____

____

◇ Be flexible, be strong. And smile! ◇

My Competition Goals:

Date: _______________

Competition name: _______________

____

____

____

____

____

____

____

____

____

COMMENTS: _______________________________________

____

◇ You can do it! ◇

My Competition Achievements:

Date: _______________

Competition name: _______________________

____

____

____

____

____

____

____

____

____

SCORES: ___________________________________

____

◇　Go for gold!　◇

My Competition Goals:

Date: _______________

Competition name: _______________

____

____

____

____

____

____

____

____

____

____

COMMENTS: _______________________________

____

◇ Dreams are possible. ◇

My Competition Achievements:

Date: _______________

Competition name: _______________

____

____

____

____

____

____

____

____

____

SCORES: _________________________________

____

◇ Flipping out is fun! ◇

My Competition Goals:

Date: ___________________

Competition name: ___________________

____

____

____

____

____

____

____

____

____

____

COMMENTS: ___________________

____

◇ Don't give up! ◇

My Competition Achievements:

Date: _________________

Competition name: ___________________

____

____

____

____

____

____

____

____

____

SCORES: _______________________________

____

◇ *Train like a champion.* ◇

My Competition Goals:

Date: _______________

Competition name: _______________

____

____

____

____

____

____

____

____

____

COMMENTS: _______________________________

____

◇   Aim high!   ◇

My Competition Achievements:

Date: _______________

Competition name: _______________

____

____

____

____

____

____

____

____

____

SCORES: _______________________________

____

◇ You're a star! ◇

My Competition Goals:

Date: _______________

Competition name: _______________

____

____

____

____

____

____

____

____

____

____

COMMENTS: _______________

____

◇ Trampolining counts as flying. ◇

My Competition Achievements:

Date: _______________

Competition name: _______________

____

____

____

____

____

____

____

____

____

SCORES: _______________

____

◇ I love trampolining! ◇

My Competition Goals:

Date: _______________

Competition name: _______________

____

____

____

____

____

____

____

____

____

COMMENTS: _______________________________

____

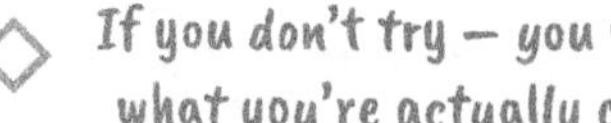

My Competition Achievements:

Date: _______________

Competition name: _______________

____

____

____

____

____

____

____

____

____

____

SCORES: _______________________________

____

◇ You got this! ◇

My Competition Goals:

Date: _______________

Competition name: _______________

____

____

____

____

____

____

____

____

____

____

COMMENTS: _______________________________

____

◇   Aim high!   ◇

My Competition Achievements:

Date: ___________________

Competition name: ___________________

____

____

____

____

____

____

____

____

____

____

SCORES: ___________________

____

◇　You're a star!　◇

My Competition Goals:

Date: _______________

Competition name: _______________

____

____

____

____

____

____

____

____

____

____

COMMENTS: _______________

____

◇ Trampolining counts as flying. ◇

My Competition Achievements:

Date: _______________

Competition name: _______________

____

____

____

____

____

____

____

____

SCORES: _______________

____

◇ *I love gymnastics!* ◇

My Competition Goals:

Date: _______________

Competition name: _______________

____

____

____

____

____

____

____

____

____

____

COMMENTS: _______________

____

◇ Trampolining is the best! ◇

My Competition Achievements:

Date: _______________

Competition name: _______________

____

____

____

____

____

____

____

____

____

SCORES: _______________________

◇ Don't forget to have fun. ◇

My Competition Goals:

Date: _______________

Competition name: _______________

____

____

____

____

____

____

____

____

____

____

COMMENTS: _______________________________

____

◇ **Run towards a challenge, not away from it.** ◇

My Competition Achievements:

Date: _______________

Competition name: _______________

____

____

____

____

____

____

____

____

____

SCORES: _______________

____

◇ Fly like an eagle. ◇

Extra notes

www.ingramcontent.com/pod-product-compliance
Lightning Source LLC
Chambersburg PA
CBHW070316120726
47910CB00007B/2504